JUST ONE MORE HUG

bookoli

Babytail the elephant loves to make her family happy.

And today she decides to be the most

helpful little elephant there ever was.

'I know,' thinks Babytail. 'I can help Mama with her daisy chain.'

But... *OOPS!*

Babytail snaps the chain in two with her trunk.

"Don't worry," smiles Mama,
and she gives Babytail a big hug.

Next, Babytail tries to help her brother pick juicy mangoes. But...

SQUISH! SQUASH!

Oh, dear. Babytail steps on his pile of mangoes and squashes them flat.

Poor Babytail feels terrible.

"It doesn't matter," says her brother,

and he gives her a big hug.

'Maybe **I** can help my sister paint her leaf picture,'

thinks Babytail. But...

ATISHOO!

Babytail sneezes and blows the leaf into the lake.

"It's only a picture,"

smiles her big sister,

and she gives Babytail a big hug.

"I don't know how to be helpful,"

little Babytail sighs.

A tear floats slowly down her cheek.

"I just make everything worse."

"Don't be sad, little Babytail," says her brother.

"Nobody minds if you make a mistake."

"We all do that sometimes,"

says her sister.

"And you are always helpful,

little Babytail," says Mama.

"You help us feel happy."

Babytail feels warm and happy inside.

"And you are the best at giving hugs," says Mama.

"Then can I give you just one more hug?"

giggles Babytail.

And with just one more hug, little Babytail falls fast asleep.